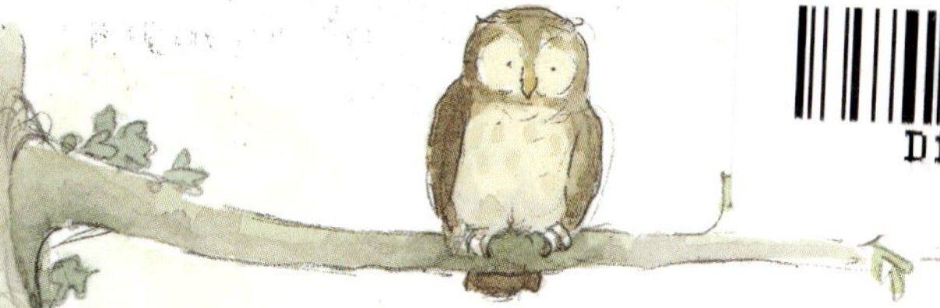

Walk in the Woods

Written by Linda Strachan

Illustrated by Priscilla Lamont

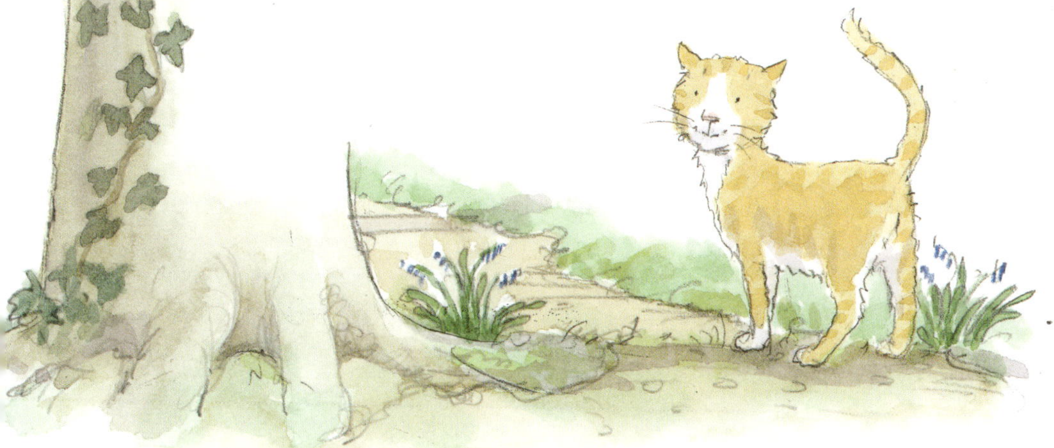

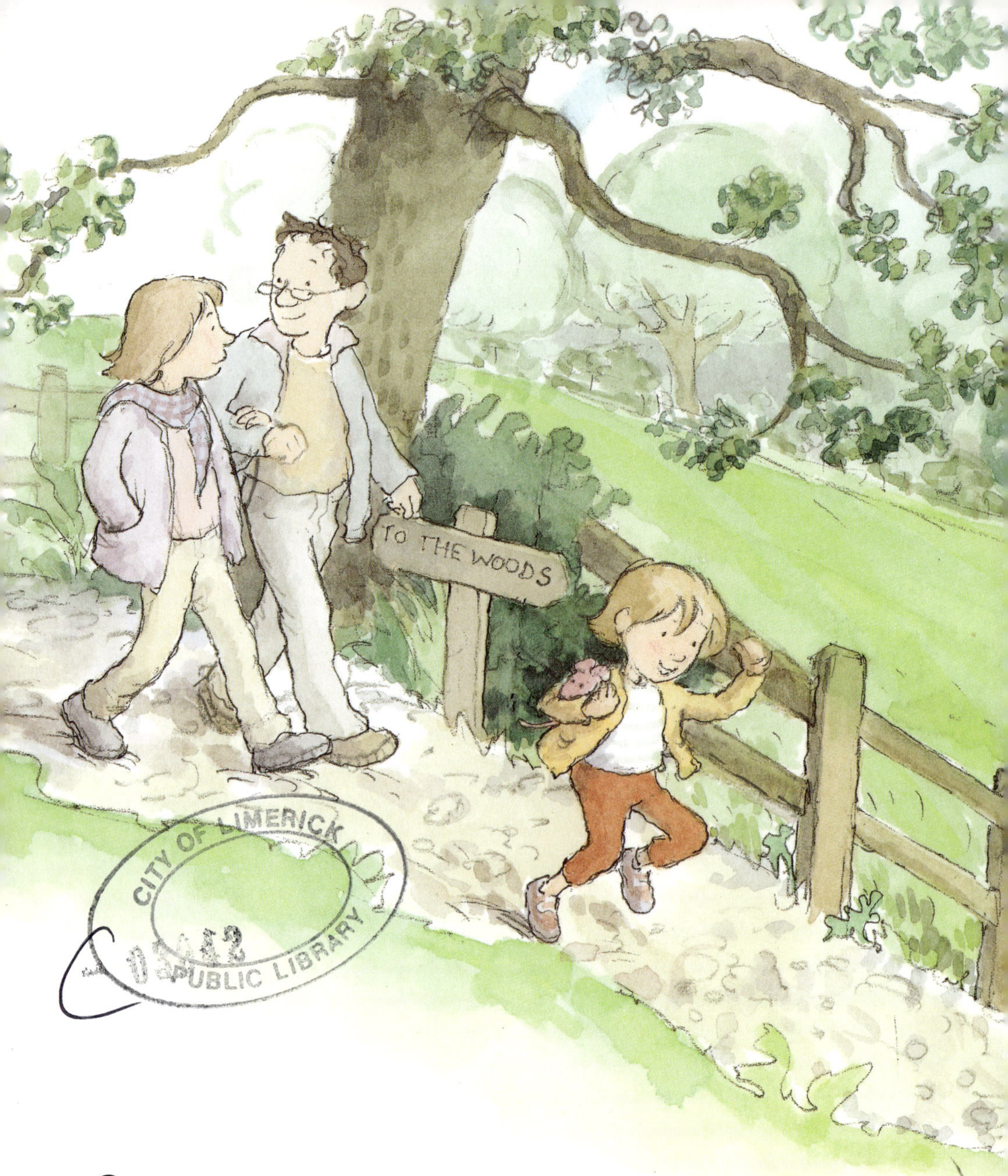
TO THE WOODS

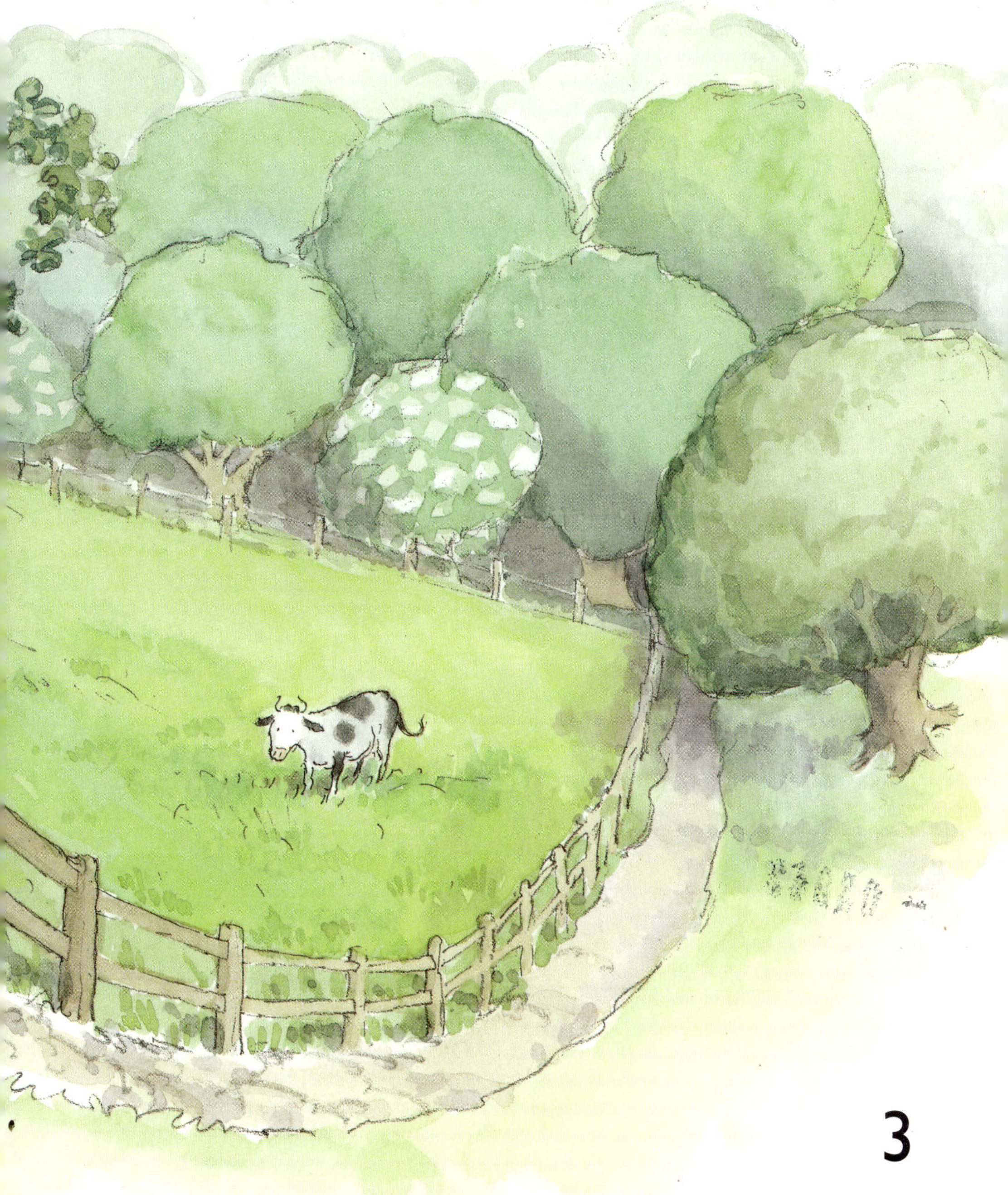

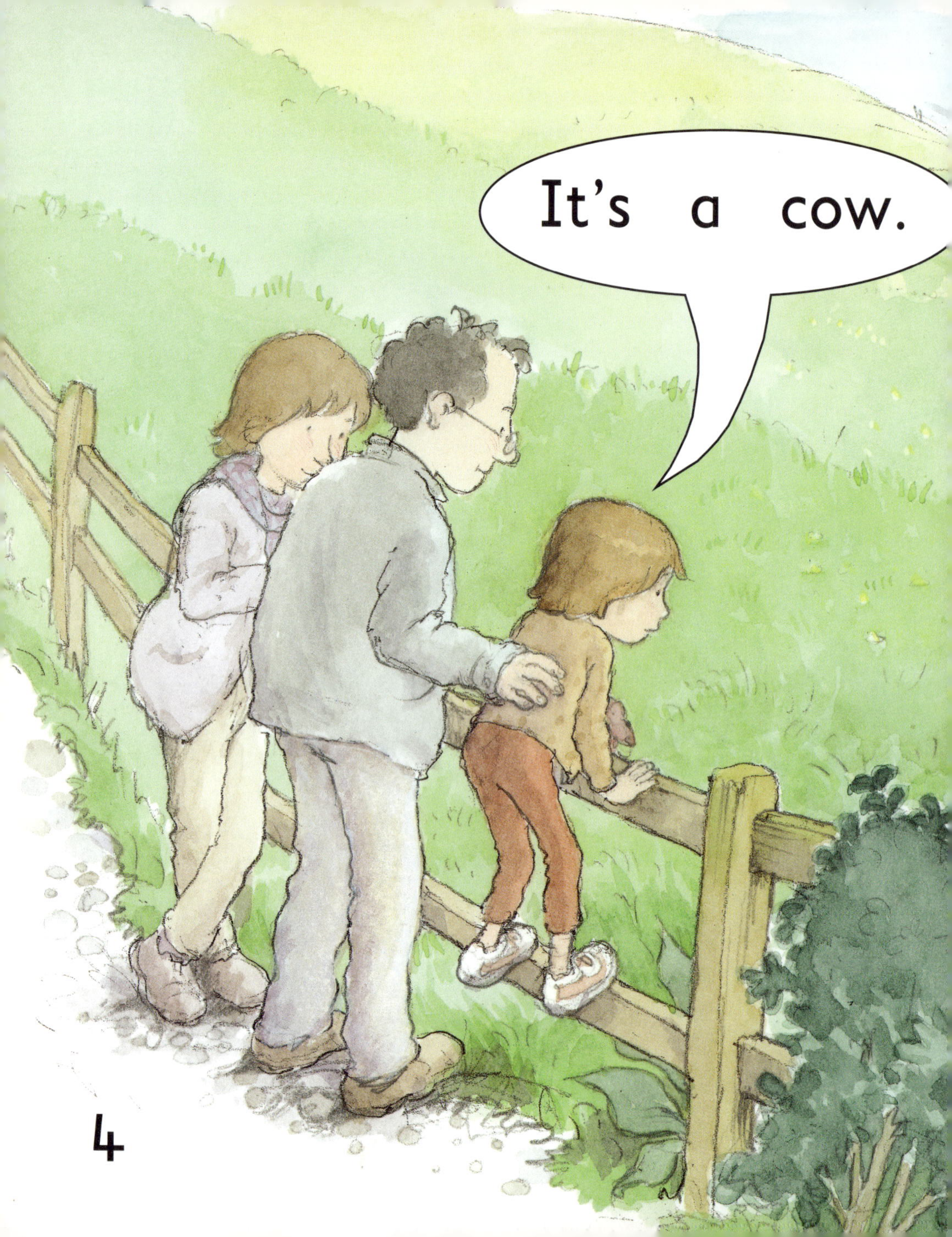
It's a cow.

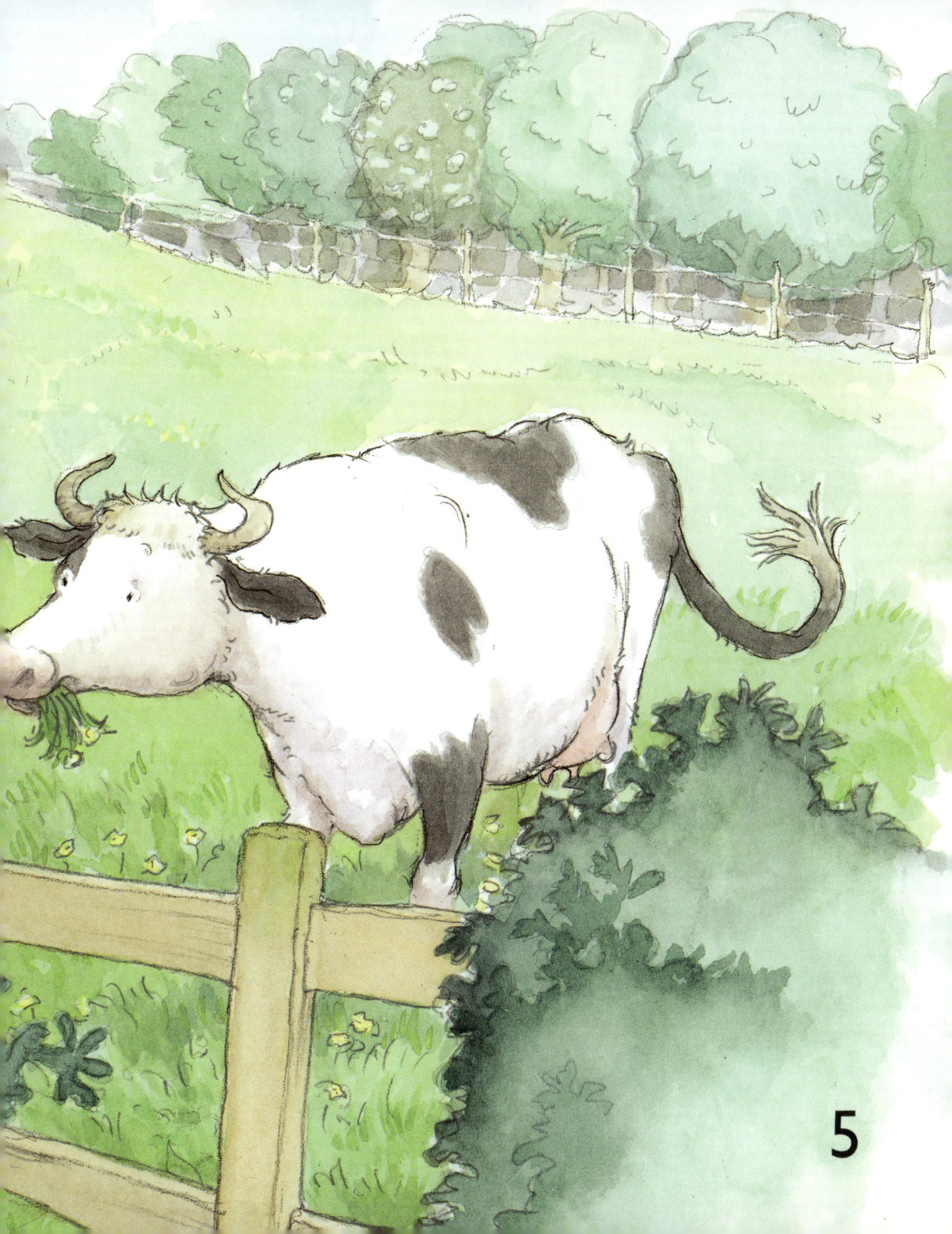

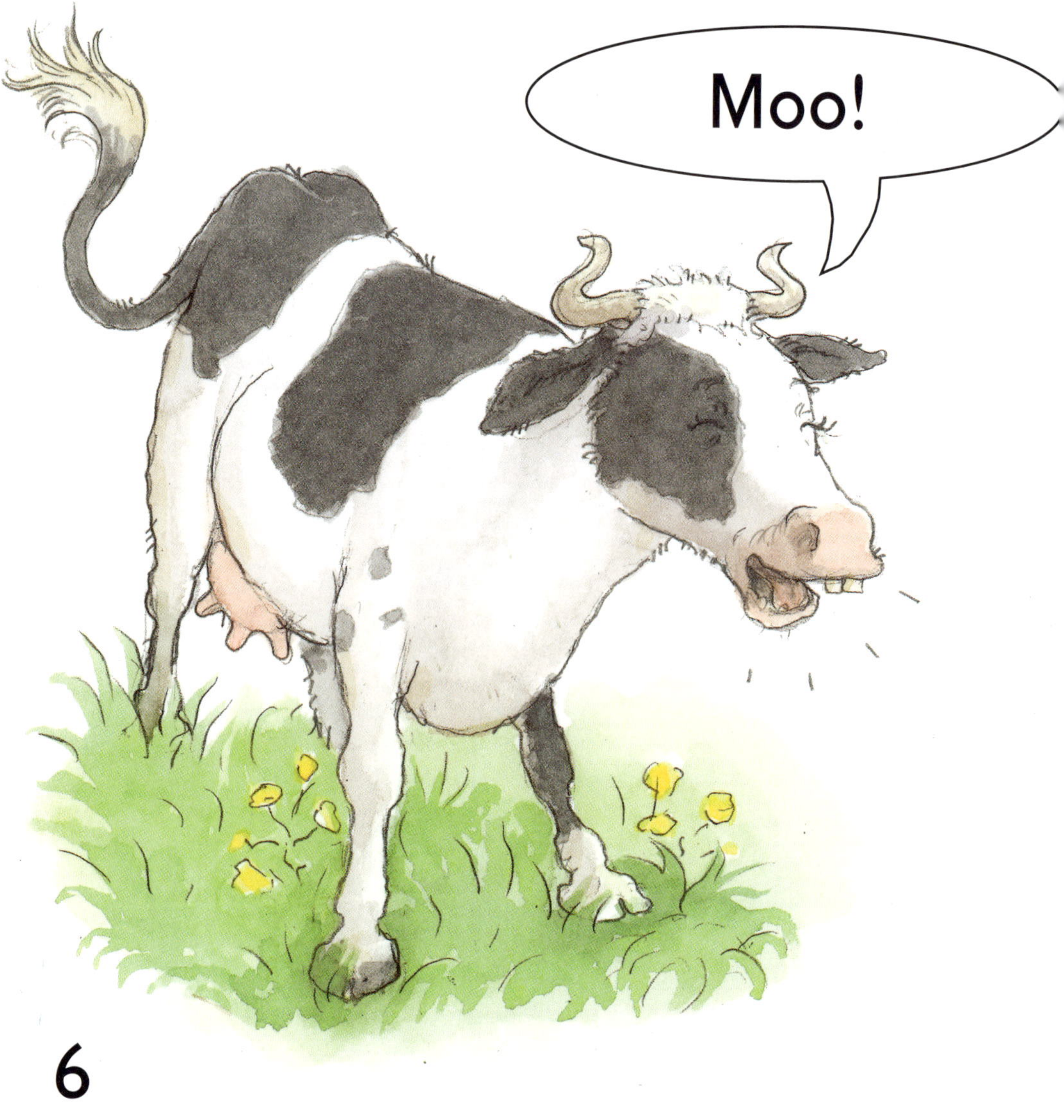
Moo!

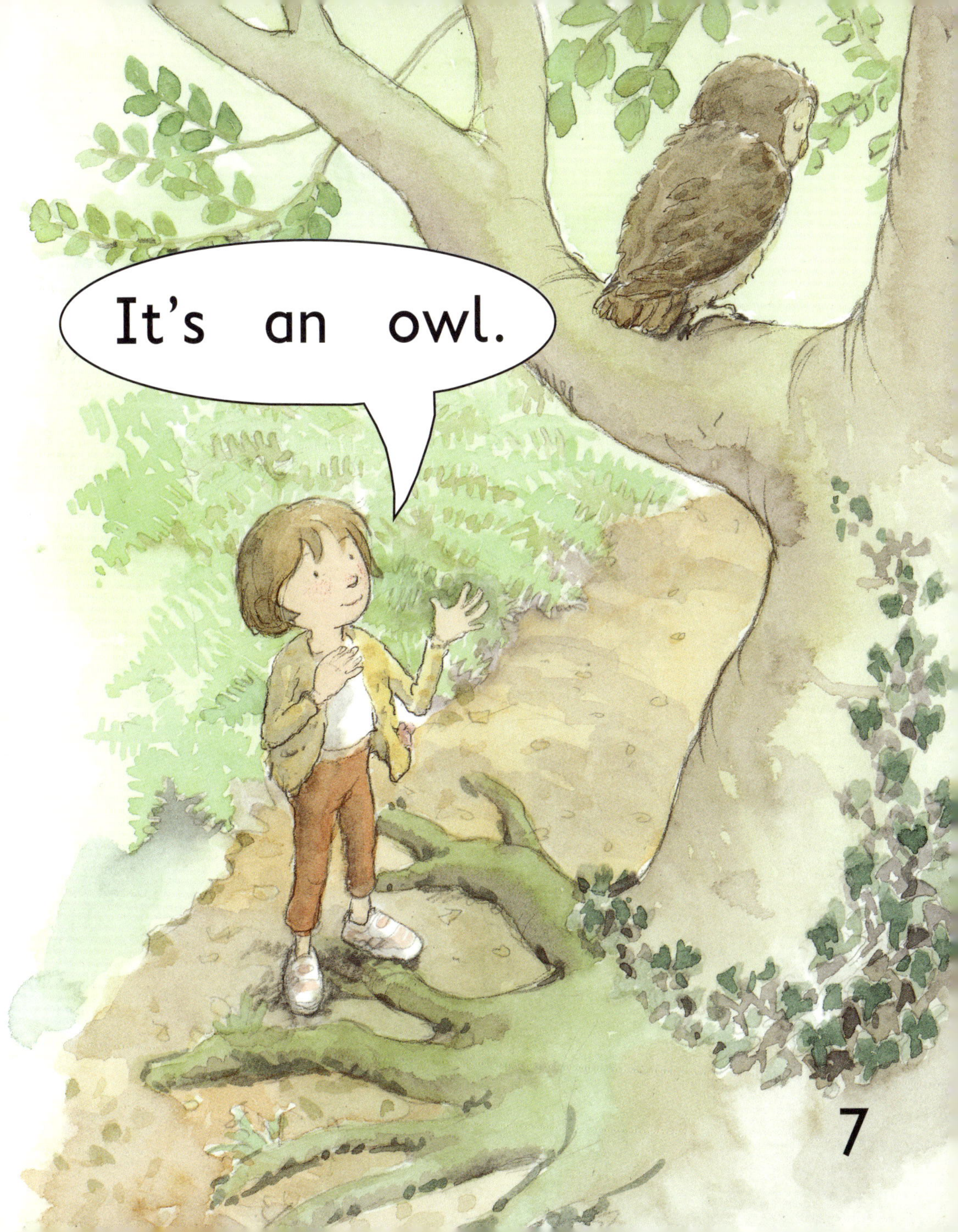
It's an owl.

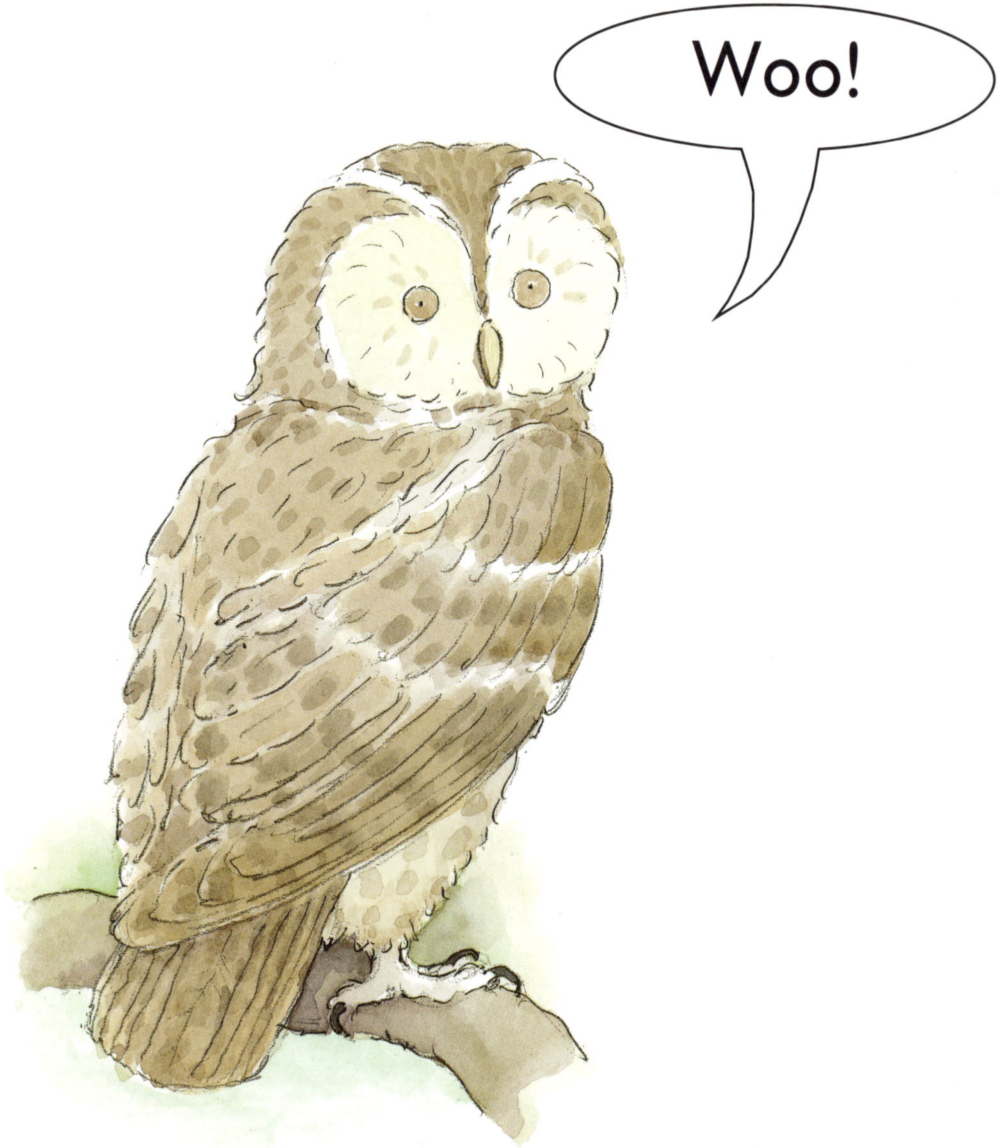
Woo!

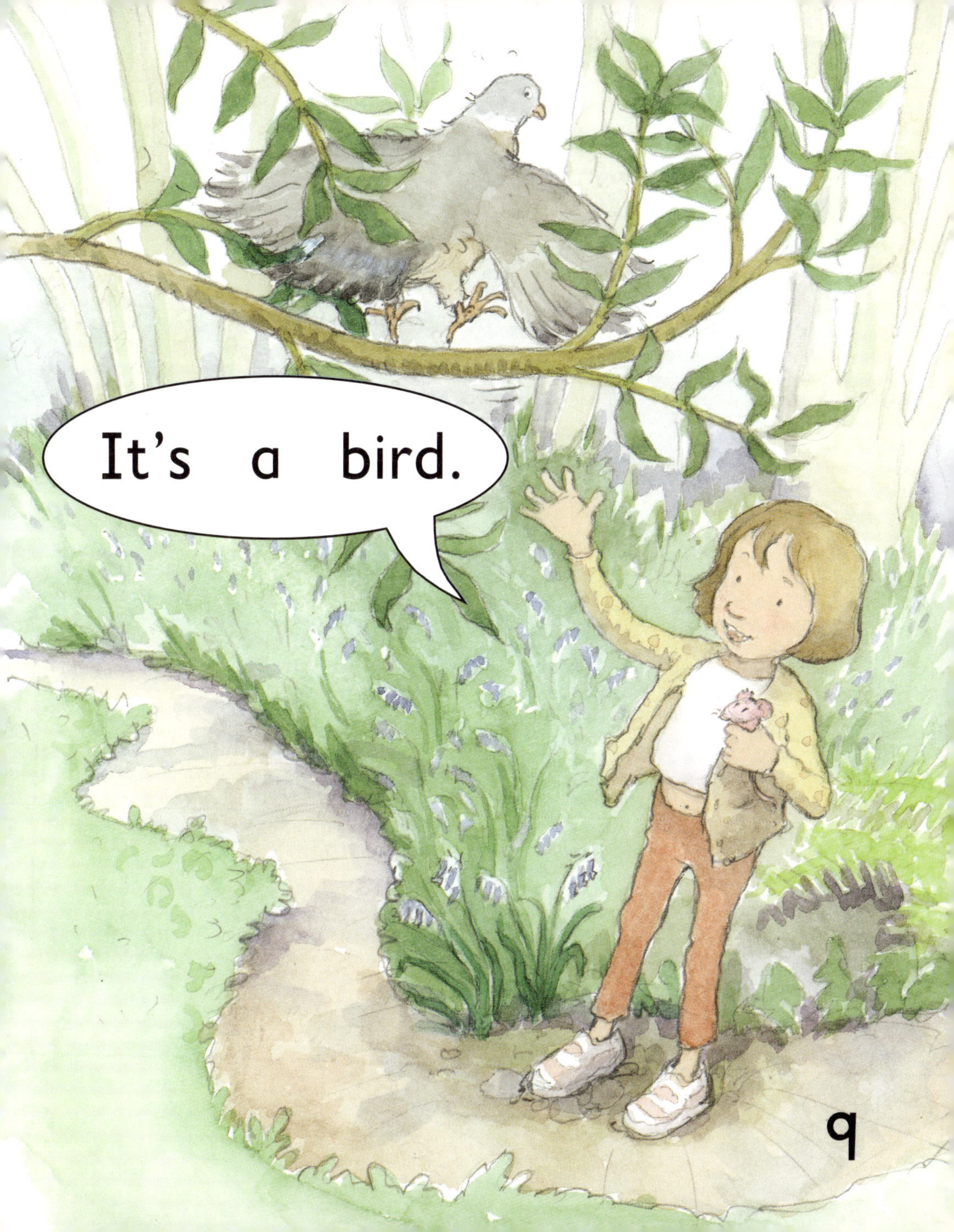
It's a bird.

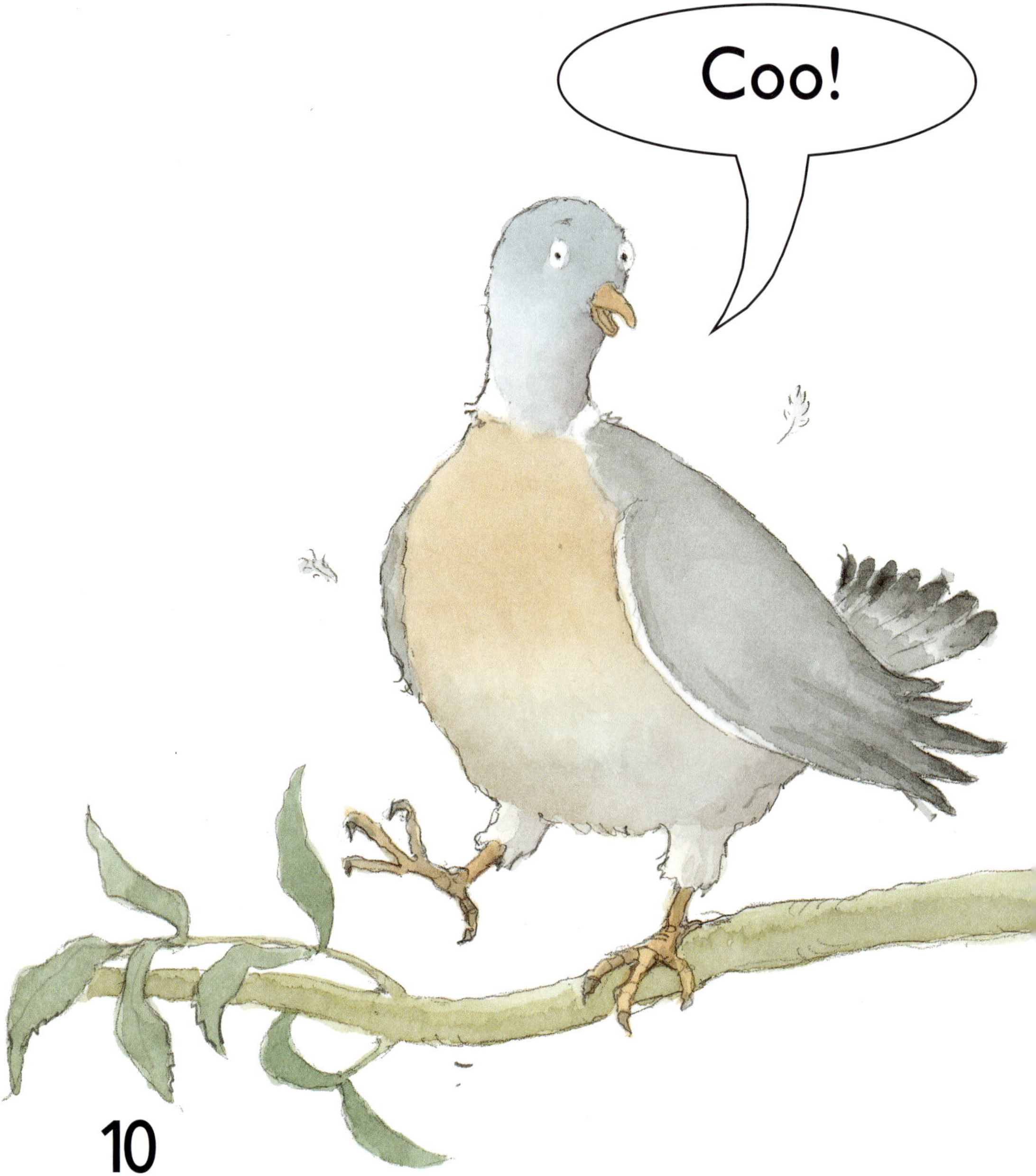
Coo!

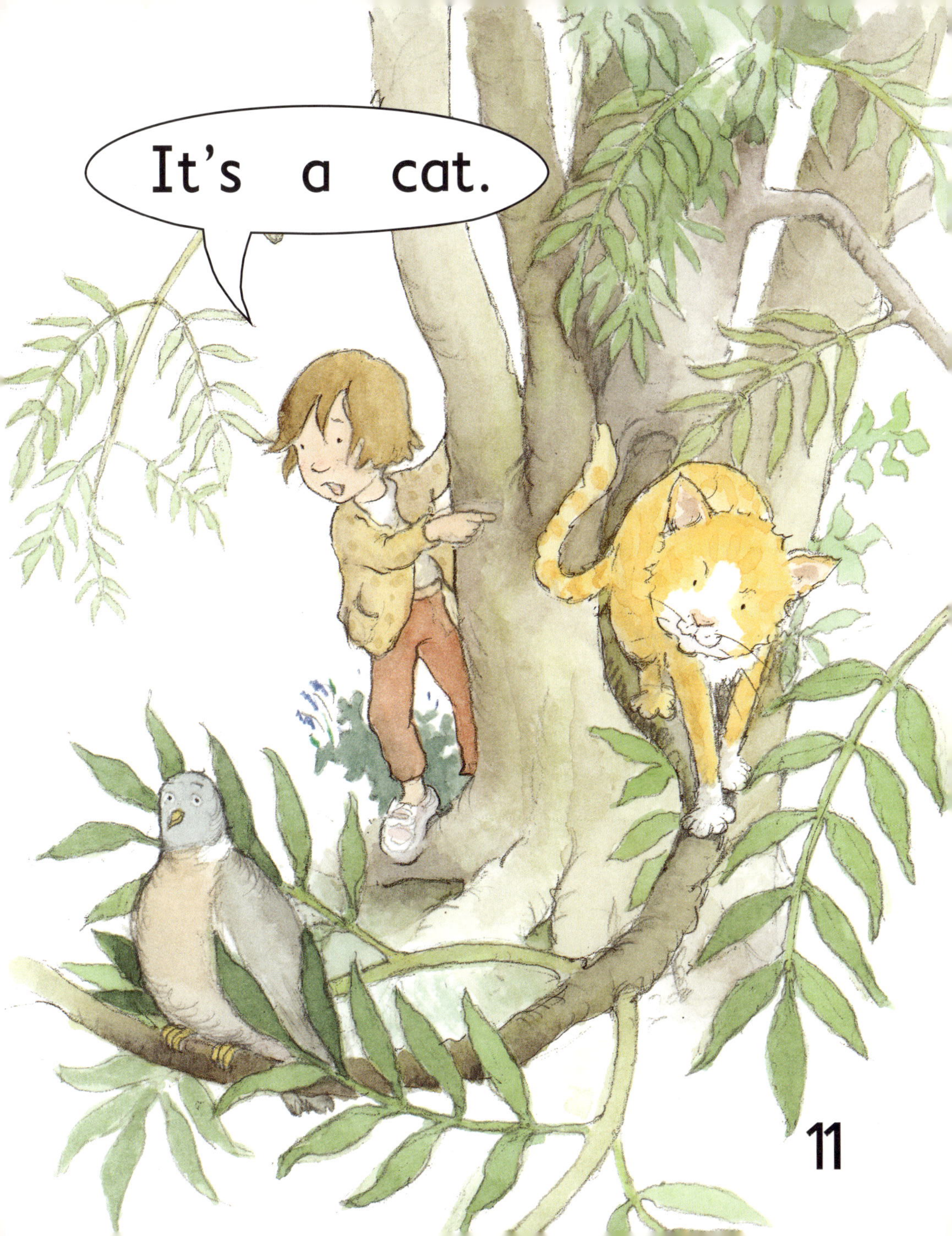
It's a cat.

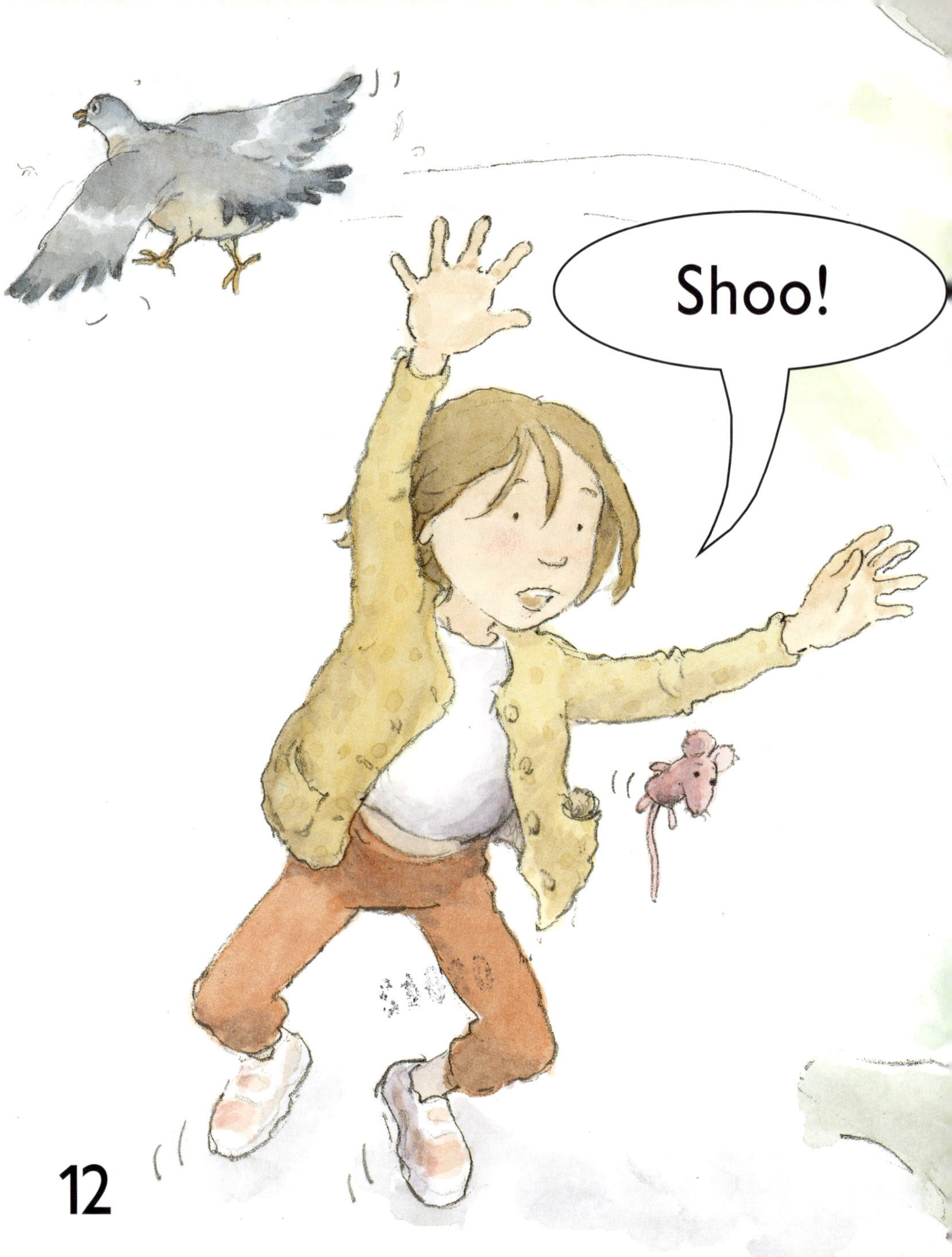
Shoo!

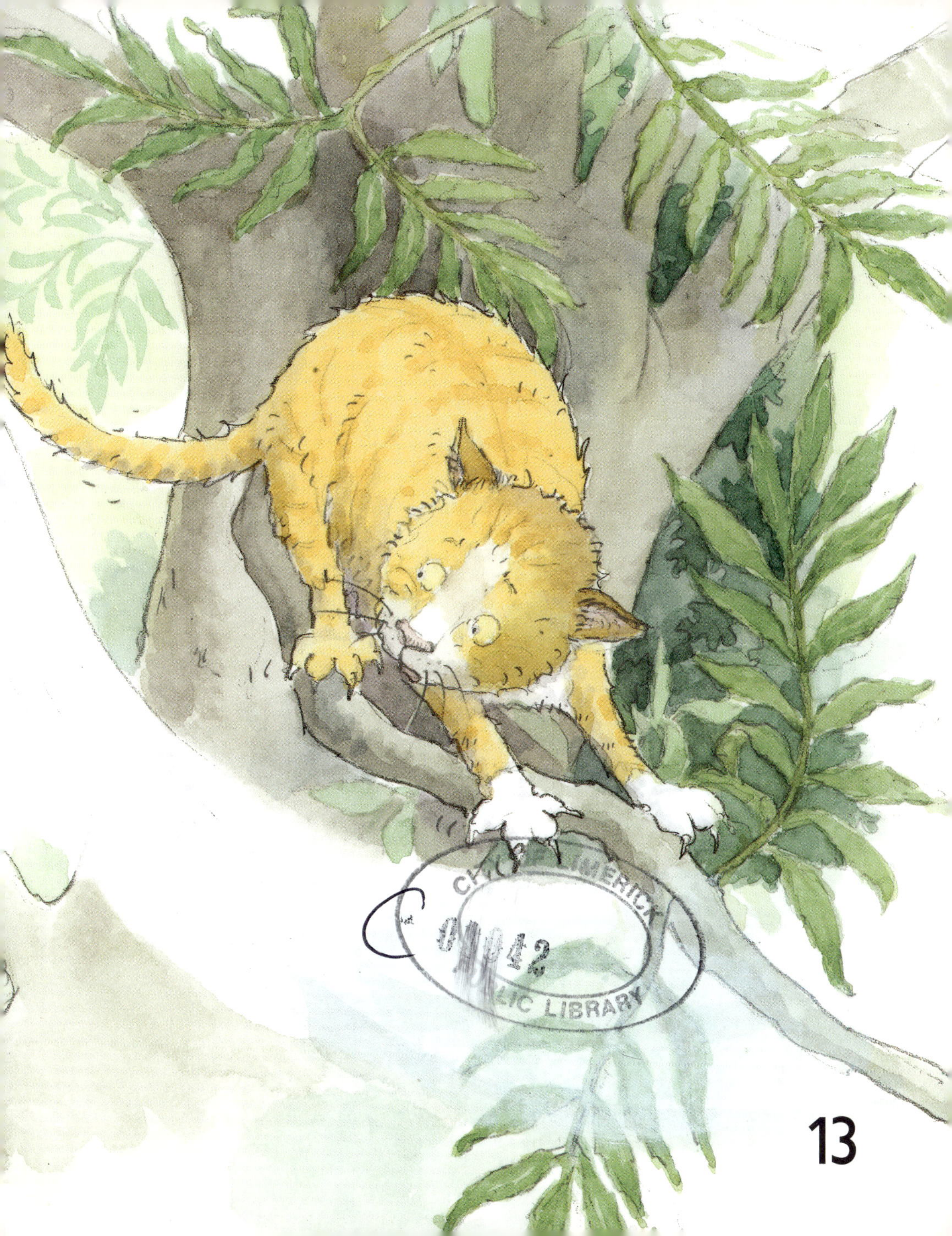

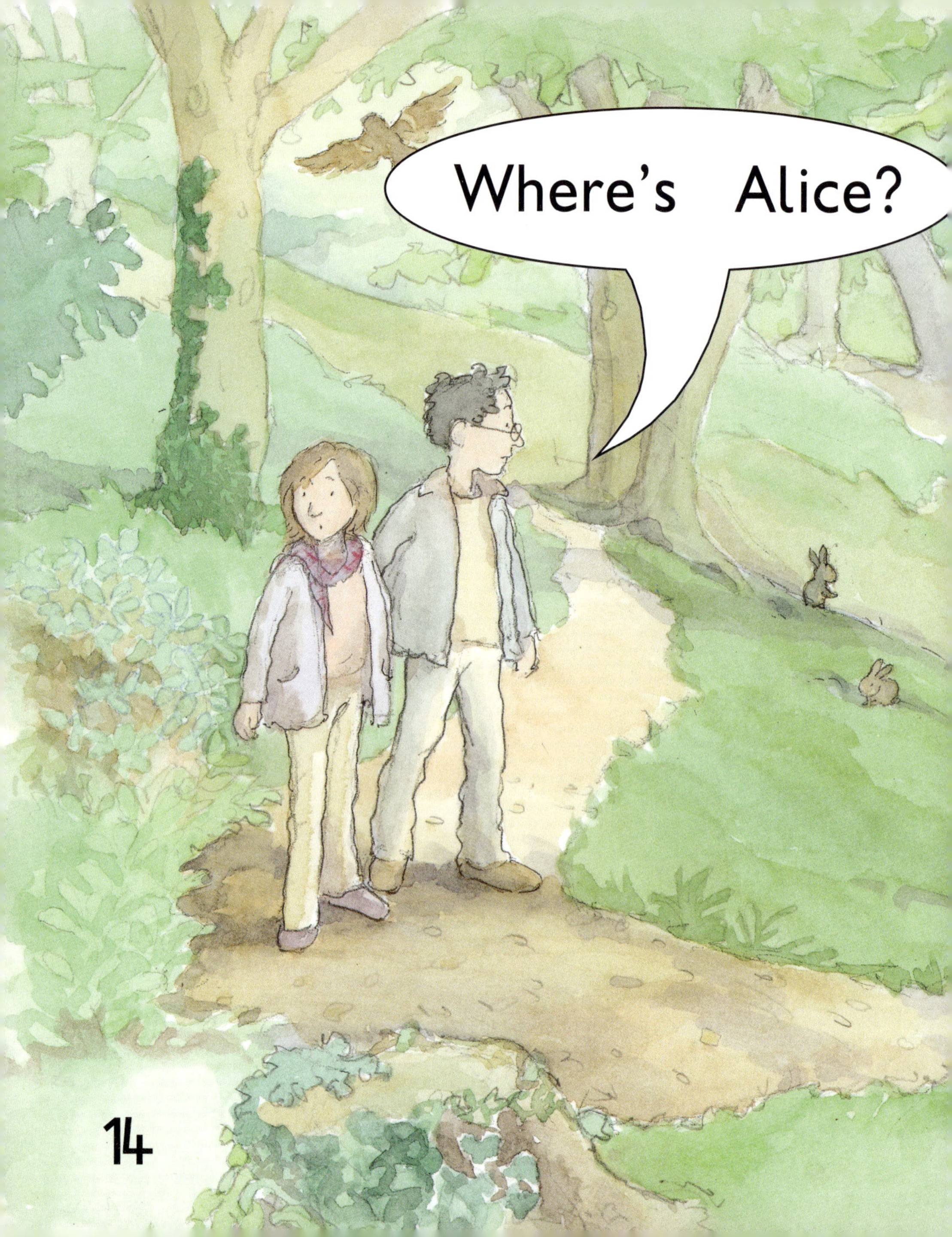
Where's Alice?

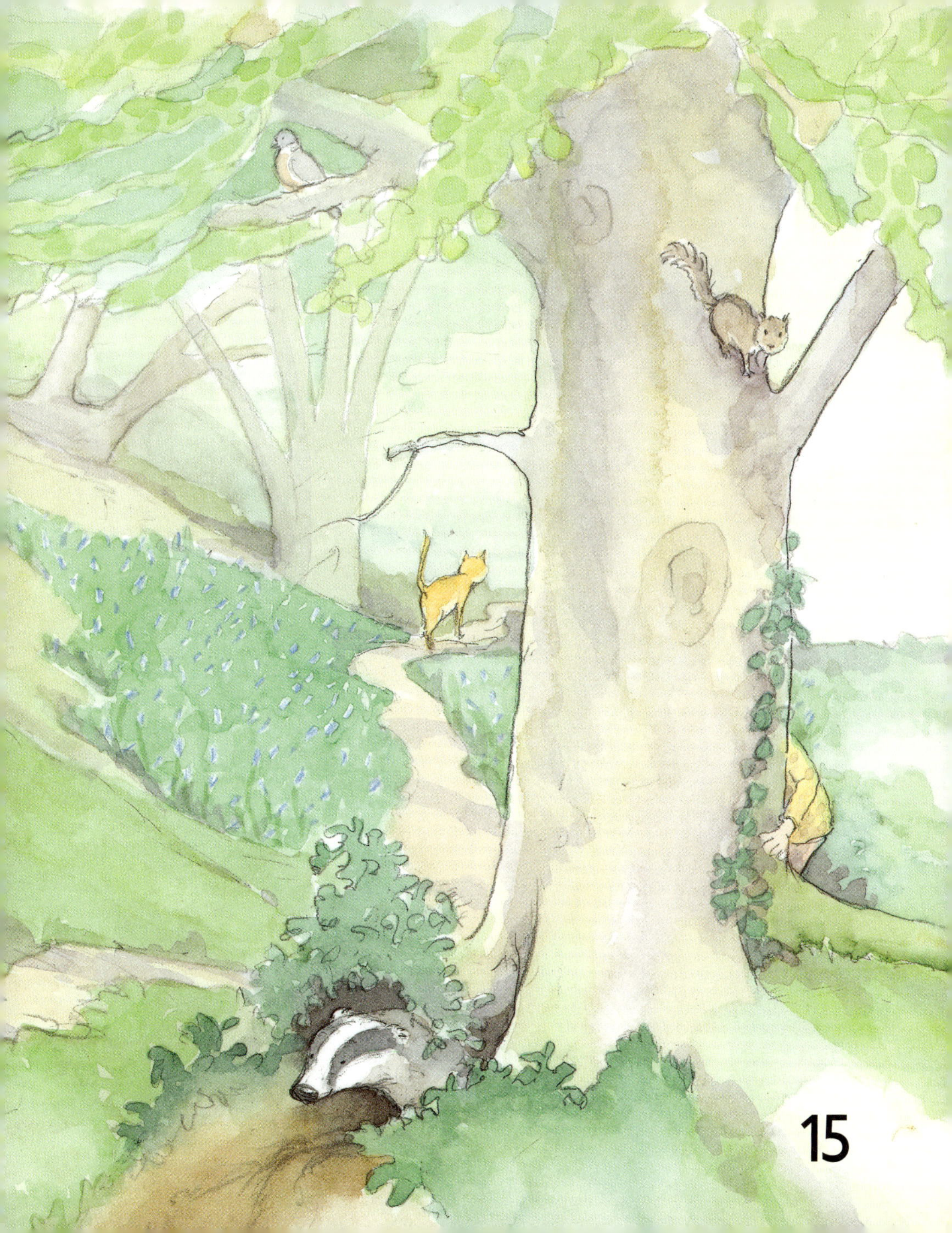

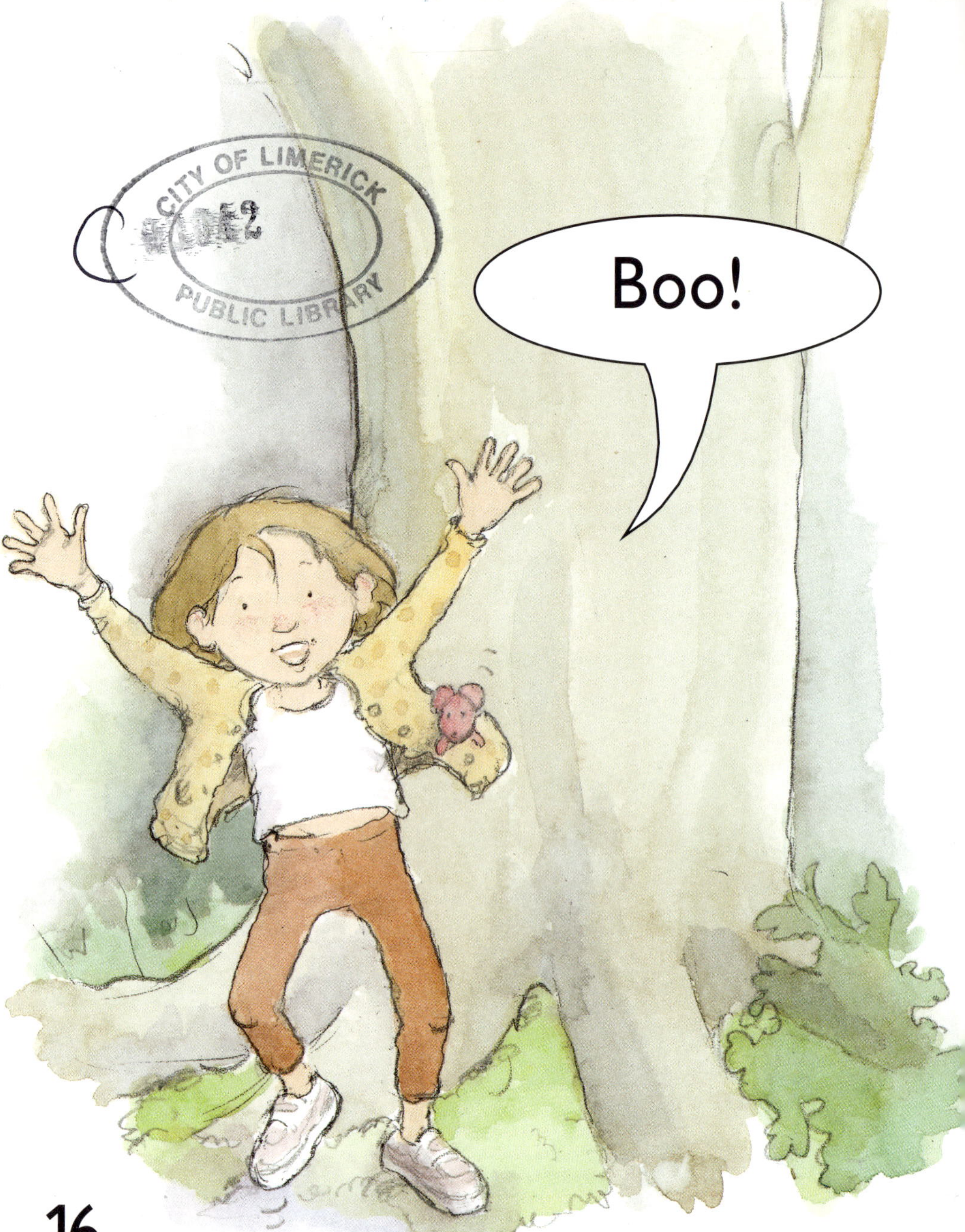
Boo!